Ladybird  Readers

On a Boat

Series Editor: Sorrel Pitts
Text adapted by Sorrel Pitts

LADYBIRD BOOKS

UK | USA | Canada | Ireland | Australia
India | New Zealand | South Africa

Ladybird Books is part of the Penguin Random House group of companies
whose addresses can be found at global.penguinrandomhouse.com.
www.penguin.co.uk   www.puffin.co.uk   www.ladybird.co.uk

Text adapted from *Peppa Pig: Going Boating*, first published by Ladybird Books, 2008
This version first published by Ladybird Books, 2017
001

This book is based on the
TV Series 'Peppa Pig'.
'Peppa Pig' is created by
Neville Astley and Mark Baker.
Peppa Pig © Astley Baker Davies Ltd/
Entertainment One UK Ltd 2003.

www.peppapig.com

Printed in China

A CIP catalogue record for this book is available from the British Library

ISBN: 978-0-241-29744-5

All correspondence to:
Ladybird Books
Penguin Random House Children's
80 Strand, London WC2R 0RL

Ladybird Readers

On a Boat

Based on the Peppa Pig
TV series

Picture words

Peppa

Mommy Pig

Daddy Pig

Daddy Elephant

Danny Dog

4

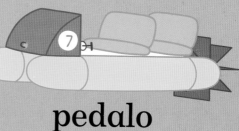

pedalo

Captain Dog

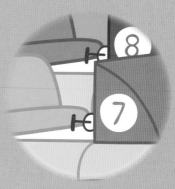

pedal

(verb)

Emily Elephant

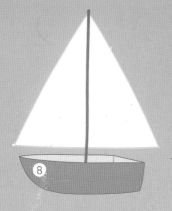

boat

Miss Rabbit

Peppa and her family
are going on a boat.

"Boats! Get your boats here!" says Miss Rabbit.

"We don't want these boats," says Daddy Pig. "These boats are small. We want a big one, please."

"These pedalos are big," says Mommy Pig.

"I would like a pedalo, please," says Daddy Pig.

Peppa and her family
are on the pedalo.

"You must pedal with your
feet!" says Miss Rabbit.

13

Emily Elephant and her family are going on a boat, too.

"We would like this one, please," says Daddy Elephant.

15

Danny Dog and Captain Dog
are going on a boat, too.

"We would like this one,
please," says Captain Dog.

The families are
on their boats!

"You must pedal,
Daddy," says Peppa.

"This is not easy,"
says Daddy Pig.

The families are hungry now.
They eat a picnic.
The children love picnics!

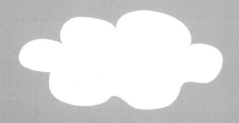

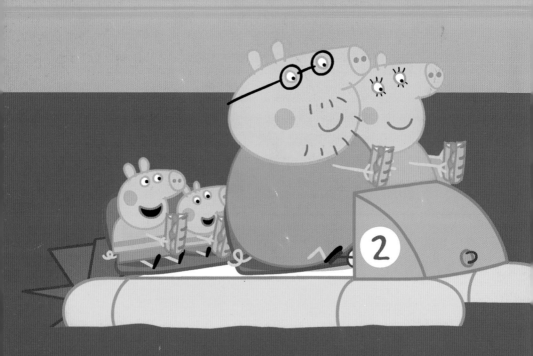

21

"Come back now!"
says Miss Rabbit.

"Who can come back
first?" says Mommy Pig.

Daddy Pig pedals
and pedals.

"This is not easy!"
he says.

Captain Dog comes
back first.

"I love going on a boat,"
he says.

Peppa and her friends love going on boats, too!

Activities

The key below describes the skills practiced in each activity.

🖊 Spelling and writing

📖 Reading

💬 Speaking

❓ Critical thinking

✦ Preparation for the Cambridge Young Learners Exams

1 Look and read. Put a ✓ or a ✗ in the boxes. 📖 ❁

1 This is Miss Rabbit. ✓

2 This is Mommy Pig. ✗

3 This is Danny Dog. ✓

4 This is Emily Elephant. ✗

5 This is Daddy Pig. ✗

2 Look and read. Write *yes* or *no*.

Peppa and her family are going on a boat.

"Boats! Get your boats here!" says Miss Rabbit.

1 Peppa and her family
see lots of boats.

2 Peppa and her family
are going on a boat.

3 "Get your boats here!"
says Mommy Pig.

4 There are three boats.

5 There are lots of trees.

yes

3 Look at the letters.
Write the words.

1   m m M y o

M o m m y Pig

2   n i c p c i

3   t o a b

4   b b t i R a

Miss

5   p p P e a

4 **Circle the correct sentences.**

1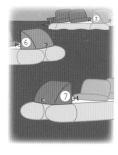

a "These pedalos are big," says Peppa.

b "These pedalos are big," says Mommy Pig.

2

a "I would like a small boat," says Peppa.

b "I would like a pedalo," says Daddy Pig.

3

a There are five small boats.

b There are four small boats.

4

a Boat 4 is orange.

b Boat 4 is yellow.

5 Find the words.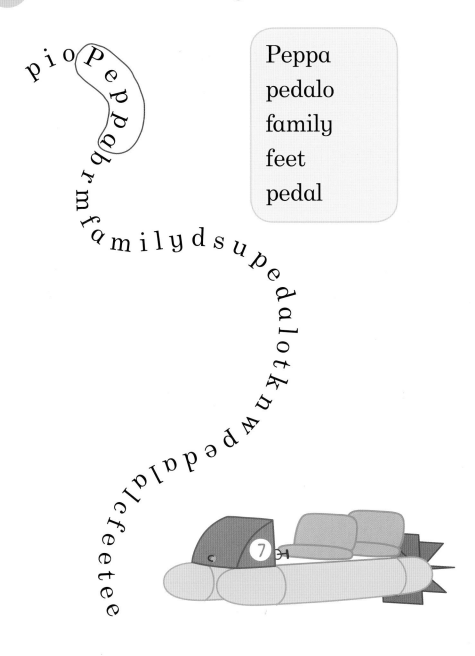

pioPeppabrmfamilydsupedalotknwpedalalcfeetee

Peppa
pedalo
family
feet
pedal

6 **Ask and answer questions about the picture with a friend.**

Peppa and her family are on the pedalo.

"You must pedal with your feet!" says Miss Rabbit.

1 Who is on the pedalo?

Peppa and her family are on the pedalo.

2 Who is sitting in front of Peppa?

3 Who is sitting next to Daddy Pig?

4 Who says, "You must pedal with your feet!"?

7 **Look and read. Choose the correct words, and write them on the lines.** 📖 ✏️ ⭐

Emily Elephant and her family are going on a boat, too.

"We would like this one, please," says Daddy Elephant.

Elephant   family   like   Miss Rabbit

1 Emily Elephant is with her mommy, daddy, and brother.

2 Emily and her .... are going on a boat, too.

3 Daddy Elephant speaks to ....

4 "We would .... this one, please," says Daddy Elephant.

8 Choose the correct words.

Danny Dog and Captain Dog are going on a boat, too.

"We would like this one, please," says Captain Dog.

1 Daddy Pig / Danny Dog is going on a boat, too.

2 He is going on a boat with **Captain Cat. / Captain Dog.**

3 "We would like this one, please," says **Danny Dog. / Captain Dog.**

4 Captain Dog likes boat **3. / 8.**

5 Boat 3 is **red. / blue.**

9 **Match the two parts of the sentences.**

1 The families are on

2 "You must pedal, Daddy,"

3 "This is not easy,"

4 The families

5 They eat

a are hungry now.

b their boats!

c says Daddy Pig.

d a picnic.

e says Peppa.

10 Circle the correct pictures.

1 They are not on a boat.

2 This is not a pedalo.

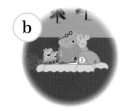

3 You must pedal this boat.

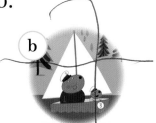

4 There are two children on this boat.

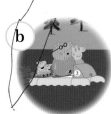

Who says this?

| Daddy Pig | Miss Rabbit | Peppa | Captain Dog |

1 "I would like a pedalo, please," says

 Daddy Pig .

2 "You must pedal, Daddy," says

 .

3 "Come back now!" says

 .

4 "This is not easy!" says

 .

5 "I love going on a boat," says

 .

12 **Order the story. Write 1—5.**

.... "You must pedal with your feet!" says Miss Rabbit.

___1___ "Boats! Get your boats here!" says Miss Rabbit.

.... Danny Dog and Captain Dog are going on a boat, too.

.... "We want a big one, please," says Daddy Pig.

.... Emily Elephant and her family are going on a boat, too.

13 **Read the text. Choose the correct words, and write them next to 1—5.**

| easy   hungry   pedal   pedalo   picnic |

Peppa's family are on their

1 ___pedalo___. Daddy Pig must

2 _____ with his feet.

But it is not ³ _____!

The families are ⁴ _____.

They eat a ⁵ _____.

14 **Work with a friend. Ask and answer questions.** 💬 ❓

1 Do you like boats?

Yes, I do.

2 Do you like big or small boats?
Why? / Why not?

3 Do you like pedalos?
Why? / Why not?

4 Do you like picnics? Why? / Why not?

15 Look at the pictures. Put a ✓
by the correct words. 📖

1

a Mommy Pig
b Peppa

2

✓ **a** Miss Rabbit ☐
b Mommy Pig ☐

3

a Daddy Elephant ☐
b Emily Elephant ☐

4

a Captain Dog ☐
b Danny Dog ☐

16 **Read the questions.**
Write the answers. 📖 ✏️

1  Who has got
lots of boats?

Miss Rabbit

2  Who pedals with his feet?

_____

3  Who says, "You must
pedal, Daddy."?

_____

4  Who comes back first?

_____

17 Write *bb*, *mm*, *pp*, or *ss*.

1 Pe p p a and her family
are going on a boat.

2 "Get your boats here," says
Miss Ra_____it.

3 "These pedalos are big," says
Mo_____y Pig.

4 "You must pedal with your feet!"
says Mi_____ Rabbit.

5 "You must pedal, Daddy," says
Pe_____a.

18 Write *boat* or *boats*.

1 "___Boats!___ Get your boats here!" says Miss Rabbit.

2 Peppa and her family are going on a _____.

3 "We don't want these _____," says Daddy Pig.

4 Emily Elephant and her family are going on a _____, too.

5 The families are on their _____!

19 **Look at the pictures. Write the correct words on the lines.**

1  This is boat .... six ....

2 This is boat ....

3 This is boat ....

4 This is boat ....

5 This is boat ....

Level 1

Anansi Helps a Friend
978–0–241–25409–7

Cinderella
978–0–241–25407–3

The Enormous Turnip
978–0–241–25408–0

On the Farm
978–0–241–25413–4

Cars
978–0–241–28354–7

Jon's Football Team
978–0–241–25411–0

The Magic Porridge Pot
978–0–241–25406–6

In the Garden
978–0–241–26220–7

Fun with Old Things
978–0–241–26219–1

Fairy Friends
978–0–241–28351–6

Peter Rabbit Goes to the Island
978–0–241–25415–8

Topsy and Tim Go to the Zoo
978–0–241–25414–1

Topsy and Tim Go to the Farm
978–0–241–28355–4

The Fair
978–0–241–28357–8

Daddy Pig's Old Chair
978–0–241–28356–1

Rex the Big Dinosaur
978–0–241–29741–4

Peter Rabbit and the Radish Robber
978-0-241-29742-1

Topsy and Tim Go to London
978–0–241–29743–8

On a Boat
978–0–241–29744–5

Baby Animals
978–0–241–29745–2

Now you're ready for Level 2!